I0817907

Nigh

book 2

Written by

Marie Bilodeau

Cover Design by Designs by Lynsey
www.designsbylynsey.co.uk

Editing by Linda Poitevin
www.lindapoitevin.com

First edition

ISBN
978-0-9940439-5-5

S&G Publishing
PO Box 30063
Greenbank North PO
Ottawa, ON
CANADA K2H 1A3

To *Katherine Gallant* of the Graham Clan,
for being so freaking awesome.

(When you're on my Faerie Apocalypse Survival Team,
I expect healthy well-balanced meals every day.
Show them how to do apocalypses right.)

Come away, O, human child!
To the woods and waters wild,
With a fairy hand in hand,
For the world's more full of weeping than
you can understand.

- William Butler Yeats, The Stolen Child -

Nigh

book 2

Written by

Marie Bilodeau

Chapter 1

THE COUNTRYSIDE stretched around them, patches of mist clinging to orchards and creeks. Alva Viola Taverner kept Percival rolling at a good clip, her mind clouded with grief and fear. Her best friend had just… *vanished*. Gone. In an instant, without any warning or the chance to say good bye.

She slowed down, glanced at the time. She'd driven at least half an hour without really paying attention to where she was going. No one had said a word. Gruff sat pale and gray beside her, still struggling with the injuries from the tow truck crash. In the rearview mirror, Hector Henry Featherson looked grim but determined. Her little sister Pete's eyes were red, but fresh tears no longer escaped them.

She realized that she had zoned out, they had all zoned out, because the world looked relatively normal right now. There were no dead bodies on the ground, the sun wasn't melting them, and the mists weren't encroaching.

She took a deep breath, not sure if the scent of lavender clung to the air or she was imaging it. She could taste the tang of iron from the school bus. Or, rather, from the people who had been inside.

She tightened her grip on the steering wheel, let the breath escape.

The radio was still on, providing slight static like distant bees. She turned the dial, trying to see if any of the local stations worked. More bees.

The static grated her nerves so she shut off the radio. Only the sound of Percival's wheels on the pavement filled the car. Al took another deep breath, then stopped mid-inhale. Had she heard a scream?

She listened intently. No one else in the car shifted. After a few more moments of silence, she let her breath escape.

The straight road barely required her attention, and Al focused on the mists instead. They might have looked innocuous if not for her memories and their shimmer. Like clumps of sugar in

cotton candy, darker than the rest and more opaque. They coated several trees, like grand ballroom dresses.

She hated the fact that the mists were pretty. It was an insult to everyone who'd perished.

Everyone.

The sight of Steve and his extended mouth flashed in her mind. Her vision blurred and her stomach flipped.

She pulled over and stopped.

"What are you doing?" Hector asked immediately. Gruff raised an eyebrow at her. Pete just kept staring out the window. She gave herself a few moments to refocus. Her mouth was dry.

"We need a plan," Al said. "We can't just keep driving without a destination. Where do we go?" She glanced at Hector in the rearview mirror.

But it was Pete who spoke up first. "We just… left her."

Al turned in her seat and looked at Pete. She wanted to reach out and grab her hand, to comfort her. But she didn't know how to cross the gap between her and her sister. Molly had always been the one to bring them together. To fill the quiet spaces with laughter, the gray days with stories. And now, Molly was the one increasing that gap.

"We'll come back for her, Pete. Once we know how to help her." She spoke with certainty, not giving herself room to question her resolve, nor looking at Hector for confirmation.

Pete gave the slightest nod, her hazel eyes rimmed with black eyeliner.

Beside her, Gruff's breathing was laboured. Despite his assurances, he wasn't getting any better, and Al's worry for him increased tenfold. She put her hand on his forehead, his skin cold and clammy. She squeezed his shoulder gently and he gave her a slight smile. But she could see that losing his wife and then Molly, on top of the accident, was taking its toll. He needed actual medical attention, not a half-assed patch job done on the side of the road.

"Can we risk going to a hospital?" Al asked Hector.

He shrugged. "Everyone will be there. The casualties will have been massive. Besides, they know how your world works. They probably made sure to take out as many emergency services as possible in the first strike." He looked toward the fields.

"The mists are less spread out," Al said. "That's good, right?" She paused, waited a beat, and asked the question that sparked hope in each of them. "Is it over?"

Hector looked down to the watch he still held. The silence in the car grew as thick as the mists had been. He looked back up, caught Al's eyes and looked away before forcing himself to hold her gaze.

"I couldn't make it stick. I was too late."

She tried to assimilate the words, and found that she couldn't.

"Does that mean there are still monsters in the mists?"

"No. The mist helped form them and bring them through. Like a door lined with curtains, their fabric flapping everywhere as too many people crossed through. The mist itself was never a monster.

It just set them free."

A pause. Nobody else spoke. Al grasped at one last straw.

"So, there are fewer monsters now?"

Hector managed to keep his eyes on hers as he answered, a whisper laced with a lifetime of regret.

"No. It just means that they've almost all crossed over. They could be anywhere, now."

Al let the words wash over her. The fear that gripped her heart cracked away into a more lasting terror, her body already tired from burning too much adrenaline for too long.

The silence lasted only moments before Pete broke it.

"Those were faeries, right?"

Hector stared at her, surprised. He looked at her as though seeing her for the first time. Pete's black-dyed long hair and intrusive makeup was a completely different look than Alva's makeup-free one, which Al supposed was the point. Pete wanted to be her own person.

But her fashion choices seemed to throw off Hector even more. He composed himself again, but not very quickly. Pete and Al shared a look, eyebrows raised, and Al felt better for it. Like she and her sister were on the same team again.

Al jumped in to save Hector from further stumbling.

"Pete, meet Hector Henry Featherson. Hector, meet Pete."

"Pleasure," he said, nodding. His mouth worked on her name and he decided not to use it. She would eventually explain the silly nickname to him, but he didn't push so she didn't offer.

"Likewise," Pete said. "Now, like Al said, we have to figure out where to go. And those were faeries, right?"

Hector nodded. "Yes. Most people wouldn't know that, I don't think. These aren't Grimms or Perrault faeries. These are the actual old faeries, from ancient tales around the world. Although, many of the tales didn't quite capture the full darkness of their essence. There weren't always survivors to relay how horrible encountering them could be."

Al looked at Pete, and waited for her to ask the next question. Obviously she knew a lot more about what was going on than Al or Gruff did. All those books lining Pete's room were coming in handy. For a second, she felt like everything was normal again. They were just chatting about something Pete had learned or was interested in, like they used to do.

A lifetime ago.

Al suddenly had the urge to ask Pete how the university visit had gone, but just as suddenly, reality crashed back down on her.

Pete wasn't going to university, because there was no more university to go to. Because Hector couldn't stop whatever was happening.

Everything they'd worked toward, every penny she'd saved and scraped for, all of it was useless. Every neighbour and neighbourhood they'd known their whole lives were more than likely gone, and they probably wouldn't ever step foot in them again. Even if they did, they would be changed beyond familiarity.

Hector and Pete were discussing some of the faeries, each more frightening than the last, but Al barely paid attention. It didn't matter what the monsters would bring, really. None of them were fighters and none of them had any special skills that would help them fight those things off.

They had a wounded old man, a young goth girl, a weird watch-making guy, and an auto tech with a big wrench.

Al gripped Percival's steering wheel and turned back to face the windshield, closing her eyes and taking a deep breath.

"… and thousands of years locked away seems to have driven some mad with the desire to be free. If the faerie queen hadn't suddenly vanished, this could have been avoided altogether…" Hector's voice droned on, Pete eating up the details.

Al focused on her breathing. On Pete's voice, growing excited by theories. On Gruff's laboured breathing.

No, they weren't anything special, but they were all she had. No matter what was happening here, no matter why this was happening, only one thing now mattered.

She looked at both of them in the rearview mirror.

"So, where do we go?" she asked again. Then added, "To be safe."

Hector nodded. "The safest place will be the land of faeries."

Pete's eyes grew wider, with excitement or fear, Al couldn't tell. Maybe both.

If mists and sunbeams could do what she'd seen them do, if her best friend could be turned into a rosebush, then did she have any choice but to accept that the land of the faeries was accessible. And safe.

"How do we get there?" she asked.

"We need an island surrounded by pure river water, or a wood with a clearing in its centre. Or a waterfall." Hector paused. "Ideally, it would be in an urban area. With more of a population. In the woods and islands, the nearby faeries might not be as… distracted by humans, making us more of a target. They might be waiting for entertainment."

Al fought a shudder of disgust at the implication and nodded. "Okay, then Fenelon Fall it is. It's in a small town not far from here. Makes sense?" She asked the last question of Pete.

She considered for a moment before answering. "It's in a small town, and not a huge fall like Niagara Falls. Will that still work?"

Hector nodded. "It should."

"Then it's settled. Gruff?" Al looked over to Gruff. His eyes were still closed, but he held up his big hand and his crooked right thumb in approval.

She steered Percival back on the road and accelerated, grateful the patches of mist weren't encroaching on them.

"How do you know all this?" Pete asked.

Hector hesitated, and Al didn't think he'd answer. But then he did, and Al discovered that despite everything that had happened

today, she could still be surprised.

"Because I just escaped from there."

Chapter 2

"YOU WERE trapped in the faerie world?" Pete asked, unable to camouflage the disbelief in her voice.

He gave her a thin smile. "Is that so hard to believe after today?"

"I guess not," she said by means of apology.

"We can go back there. The faeries abandoned it and all came here. It'll be safe for us."

"Right," Al offered. "While the cat is away, the mice will play."

"Exactly."

"What else can we expect?" she asked, wishing she had paid a bit more attention to Pete and Hector's conversation.

"I'm not absolutely certain," Hector said. "It depends on what crossed over in this exact location. All types of faeries are out. Most will be driven mad in this world. Some are angry. Others are benign. It's best that we keep moving and get to safety. Quickly."

"I thought faeries were pretty winged toys at the store," Al mumbled.

"They're nasty in old stories," Pete offered, her words coming slow and measured. She was still working through all of it. Al just nodded and let her be with her thoughts.

They could all use a bit of breathing room. Al could get them that while they drove to the Falls, at least.

"Will we be able to help Gruff there?" Al asked, meeting Hector's eyes in the mirror.

He didn't hesitate. "Yes. They have healing herbs that don't exist in this world. We can get him patched up easily."

Al flushed with relief. She couldn't bear the thought of losing Gruff. Especially not after losing Molly. Hector spoke up as though he read her mind.

"We might be able to help Molly, too."

Al looked to Pete. Her head was leaning forward, a veil of dark hair hiding most of her face, but Al knew that her sister was observing Hector through it, weighing his words and actions. She desperately wanted some time to chat things out with just her sister, to share a moment of private grief before the world swept them back up.

But they couldn't afford that luxury.

"Al," Gruff interrupted her thoughts, his tone low and laced with worry.

Up ahead, a woman walked slowly toward them, dragging her feet and stumbling on newly formed cracks in the road. Al slowed down. She could go around the woman easily enough, and probably should, given that she wasn't sure she could trust anyone. But the woman seemed so vulnerable that Al couldn't stand the idea of not at least asking her if she was all right.

The woman's car might have crashed and she might be stuck out here alone. She might need help. Al looked at the woman's bare feet, covered in dust. She definitely needed help.

"Is that a baby she's carrying?" Gruff asked. He was still pale and leaning back into his seat, but his eyes were now sharp and focused.

Pete pulled herself up between the seats. Al bit back the instinct to tell her to sit back and buckle up, focusing instead on the more immediate danger of the woman.

"She has a baby," Pete whispered. She turned to Al. "We have to stop and help her."

Hector chimed in right away. "I'm not convinced that's such a good idea."

Pete turned to him, fuming. "We don't just abandon babies and mothers on the side of the road! They're people, not monsters!"

Hector was about to say something more, but Al cut him off. "Pete's right, Hector. We at least find out if she wants help."

Pete smiled gratefully at Al, who smiled back. She didn't dare tell her sister that she thought Hector was right. She liked that Pete, even after witnessing horrors and losing Molly, still believed in helping people. It's how they had been brought up, and she would support that idealism for as long as she safely could.

But there was no need to be stupid about it, either.

She lowered her window just a crack, keeping her hand on the handle to roll it back up if necessary. She stopped but kept the car in first gear so they could take off on a dime.

"Do you need help?" Alva asked. All eyes were on the woman. She was in her early thirties at the latest, but it was hard to tell under the dust clinging to her face and hair. Sandy eyelashes framed pale gray eyes. The dirt parted to reveal a hint of light brown hair.

Despite the chilly fall weather, the mother had no coat on, just a short-sleeved, stained lacey top. Her loose jeans held in a belly that still showed some of the baby weight, but she had obviously been a thin woman before the pregnancy.

She didn't blink or speak, or change her slow pace as she walked by the car.

"Ma'am?" Al asked again. This time, the woman slowed a bit and turned to Al. She smiled, her teeth white against her dusty lips. The smile didn't spread past her mouth.

"Hello. How are you today?" She asked in a monotone voice. The emptiness in her eyes scared Al. She fought against rolling up the window.

"Do you need help?" Al repeated, her hand clutching the window handle so tightly that its plastic cut into her skin.

The woman kept smiling, her head cocking a bit to the side. "Of course not. My baby and I are just out for a walk."

"Alva…" Hector cautioned.

"We can't just leave her!" Pete hissed. Hector shook his head.

"We can't help her. Not anymore," he said softly, but he looked at Al as he said it. Pete glared daggers at him before turning back to Al. "We're not leaving without her."

Al was suddenly glad for the two-door design of her car. She was certain Pete would have jumped out otherwise. She was slightly surprised and grateful that Pete wasn't climbing over Gruff to get out.

"Pete…" Al said, trying to think what else to add. That she was scared? That she couldn't stand the thought of losing her? That there were monsters walking the streets, now?

Al knew none of the arguments would resonate with Pete, whose jaw was stubbornly set. Once her sister was convinced

something should happen, Al might as well have tried to convince the CN Tower to go for a walk. Although, she supposed, that might actually be possible now.

"Would you like to see my baby?" Al jumped at the proximity of the voice. The woman was standing right beside her window, leaning down, the smile still plastered on her face. She'd been so distracted by Pete and Hector that she hadn't seen or heard her approach.

Before Al could fathom a reply, the woman held out her baby. The bundle of blankets parted and a small gray hand broke free, reaching toward Alva. The baby screamed, white hair and a long gray nose poking out, sharp teeth sticking through its gums. Yellow eyes looked deep within her, beckoning to her. She felt herself falling into those bottomless eyes, falling away from the fear and despair, into a warmth she'd never known.

Her hand loosened and slipped from the window handle. Her mind tried to claw its way out of those eyes. She gasped for breath, the whole car spinning as she tried to tear herself away from the encroaching warmth.

Come to me, she could hear the words gripping her mind, like tendrils plugging directly into her thoughts.

She jerked her hand back up and hit the door handle, her movements clunky. The gray distorted face leaned close, pungent with decay. Someone called for her more strongly, pulling on her arm.

The baby hissed in frustration and reached for her. Something fell on her. Small pellets. Sand.

The dizziness vanished and she pushed herself away. She heard Pete screaming and Hector shouting. She pressed on the clutch and the gas, her tires spinning and screeching down the road. The woman didn't follow, simply turning to watch them go as she continued holding her baby. Or whatever the hell that had been.

Al swore she could hear its screams over that of her tires.

She slowed down a bit, and only then saw the red swelling on her arm where Gruff's large hand had squeezed in an attempt to snap her back. It had felt like just an instant, but she'd lost a few minutes. Sand speckled her clothing, where Hector had thrown it to break the faerie's hold on her mind. She looked at Gruff with big eyes, saw the fear in his, and focused back on the road.

Suddenly, Fenelon Falls seemed terrifyingly far.

Chapter 3

HECTOR LOOKED down at the watch, the metal cool in his hands. Threads of understanding laced his thoughts together. He hadn't felt this certain of anything since the day he'd proposed to Stella.

They wouldn't all make it to the faerie world. Some might. Pete and Alva, he hoped. But he was no longer certain.

His plan had been simple. Restart the watch and stop the veil from failing. But it was too late, now. He had always been too late, as the faerie queen had desperately tried to get him to understand. Tried to get him to build a watch more powerful than this broken one.

A watch linked to her lifespan, and not Stella's.

He wrapped his fingers around the watch. Ten twenty-four. That was the time it would forever mark. Nothing, not even his despair to save Stella's children, could change that. He accepted it, let it wash over him, and vanish beyond fear.

He had almost lost Alva again. As simple as that. A moment in time, a single faerie. Worse, he was almost out of sand. He had put what extra he could in his pockets, to ward off faerie magic. He shifted, uncomfortable. He'd also sewn sand into the lining of his coat and in the sole of his boots, to keep time from finding him. He could never step fully on the ground of this earth again, lest he turn to the dust of a century.

He could use the sand protecting him, but he would forfeit his life.

He was a watchmaker no longer able to survive the speed of his own time.

Hector imagined the ticking of the watch. He imagined it like heartbeats, mimicking his own. A beat per second. Tiny gears working away diligently, keeping their one task. To move time forward. To succeed at one thing, like a soldier on the field.

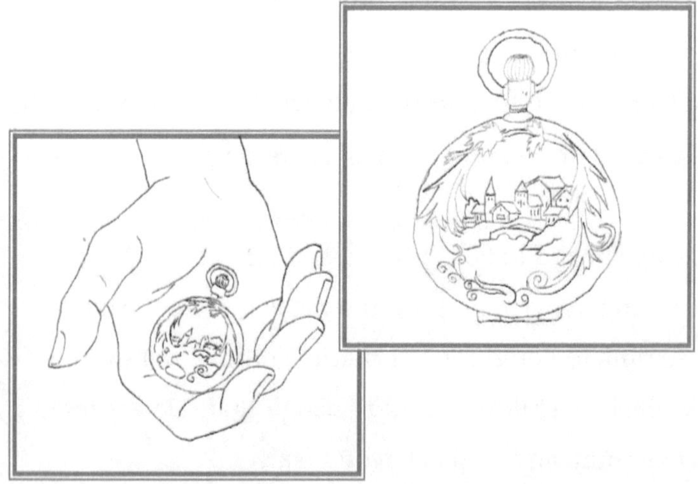

He would use the sand if he needed to. He would turn to dust in this world.

But not before he answered one final battle call.

Percival's motor sputtered and white smoke wisped out from under the hood.

"No, no, no," Al said under her breath as the gas line stopped feeding the engine and the orange muscle car just drifted along until coming to a complete stop.

"Engine not up to speed?" Gruff asked.

Al shook her head. "Maintained regularly, built most of this myself… you know as well as I do that Percival shouldn't just be stopping."

"It's been through a lot. Maybe something got into it?"

Al's skin crawled and she wanted to throw herself out of the car.

"We could walk," Pete offered from the back. But Hector shook his head.

"We're safer in here. The iron in this car is going to keep some of the faeries at bay. It's not much protection, but it's certainly better than nothing at all."

"Besides, Gruff's in no condition to walk," Al added before Pete could bring up another argument.

"Well, can we at least stretch? This back seat isn't very

comfortable."

"I'm going to have a look to get us going again," Al said, grabbing Big Bertha from the back seat, swallowing bile as she remembered Molly gripping it tightly, menacing Hector. "You can stretch, but no wandering."

"Fine," Pete said.

Al stood up and popped the hood, waving away the acrid smoke. Everyone scrambled out of the car, even Gruff. He joined her up front and she was about to tell him to go sit back down when he waved her off with his good arm.

"I need to move too, Al. You keep treating me like I'm dying and I'm going to start believing it."

Al bit back her reply and nodded. The old mechanic leaned near the engine and whistled. "Nice. I haven't looked in here since your dad… well, you sure did a great job maintaining Percival," he finished softly. "Your dad would be proud of you, Al."

Al swallowed hard. Hearing about her dad made everything worse. His life, and death, seemed to belong to another life, now. Another time, so far away that Al could never return there. She wondered if his tombstone had fallen. And if it mattered at all.

She gripped the edge of Percival's chassis and focused on the problem at hand.

"Okay, so, perfectly healthy engine clunks out for no reason after running away from evil faerie creatures of death. What's our protocol for that?"

Gruff snorted and Al grinned at him. Hector lingered near the hood, looking at the engine.

"Might be something in the fluids," he offered. "If a faerie managed to hop a ride, it's probably dead from all the iron. What could clog up?"

Al looked at him for a second before exchanging a look with Gruff. "Well, she sputtered, so maybe gas? And smoked, so maybe the oil? Do these things like gasoline and oil?"

Hector shrugged. "I don't think they know enough about this world anymore to know what they like. But most faeries are linked to an element, like water, so examining fluids seems like a reasonable place to start."

"Or, maybe this isn't faerie related at all," Al offered, hoping to find a mundane explanation for her car troubles. A faerie infiltrating Percival seemed infinitely more personal than a faerie infiltrating her home.

"Let's check the fluid lines first, just in case," Gruff offered gently. Al sighed.

"Run-of-the-mill car troubles would just be really nice today," she mumbled.

She checked what she could of the feeds. She had her tool box in the trunk and could do quite a few repairs on the road, but the thought of jacking up Percival and being that vulnerable under a car wasn't very appealing.

"Oil?" Gruff asked. Alva pulled the dipstick out, screamed in surprise, and dropped it. It wasn't honey coloured, as it should have been. It was blood red.

"That seems to be the problem," Hector said. Al almost bit off his head, but was thrown when she saw a half smile on his lips. That was something new.

"Glad you find this funny," she muttered instead.

"What the hell is in there?" Gruff asked, perking up at the mystery.

"You find this funny too?" Al asked, but leaned in to check nonetheless. Slowly, in case something decided to jump out.

"If babies can try to eat your soul," Al mumbled, "then I don't want to know what something turning oil to blood might do."

"It's probably a dead faerie," Hector offered. "Might have, um, lost its final meal dying in there. A water faerie can change fluid consistency."

Pete had scooted closer, obviously listening but looking out at some mist in a tree in the field. The fields were empty, already having borne this year's crops. Only the scattered trees, marking property lines, remained. The mist clung to them like spider webs.

"Great. Wonderful."

Al could see something floating in the liquid. She took a deep breath, picked up the dipstick, and stuck it in. She managed to pierce the object through and pull it out. It was a dark wing, starlight trapped in it, shimmering despite the oil.

"It's beautiful," Pete said, coming closer.

"It ate someone," Al said, swinging the wing away.

"Might have just been part of someone," Hector offered.

"Wonderful," she muttered as she capped off the oil. "I'm going to have to change the oil. I have some in the trunk, but I'm going to try to do this without jacking up the car, so we can make a quick escape if we need to."

"Can't escape quick without oil, Al," Gruff said. Al went to the back and snatched up her tools and supplies. She could try topping it off, but the oil was already full, and she feared the whole thing was blood by now.

She crouched beside Percival. Damn low riding car. She couldn't access the oil easily without jacking it up at least partway. Well, she'd just have to make it fast.

She set her parking brakes, grabbed the jack and pumped the front of the car up as quickly as she could. Hector and Pete wandered away from the car. Gruff looked at Percival, as though willing the oil to change back from blood.

Now that they were stopped, Al noticed that the mists weren't stationary. They were dancing around the trees, in a slow embrace, shifting slowly toward them.

She pumped faster.

Hector kept an eye on the youngest Taverner sister as Al crawled under her car to fix it. He should have worried more about a faerie finding the fluid lines of the car, but he'd been so wrapped up in the individual moments of survival that he hadn't thought ahead enough. It could get them all killed. But so could have splitting his attention.

He cast aside his worries as useless. Alva had to concentrate on working as quickly as possible so that he could get them to the faerie world. Seeing her jump back at the sight had made him laugh, her wide eyes so much like Stella's.

"How long were you there?" Pete suddenly asked. Hector stared at her overdone appearance for a few moments before clearing his throat and answering.

"Depends," he said carefully. Lying to her wouldn't change facts, and Pete had already shown she knew enough faerie lore to deduce whatever Hector didn't tell her.

She examined him, her hazel eyes intense. The dark makeup around her eyes made her seem older than she was, but her soft skin betrayed her younger age. She seemed paler due to her black hair. He imagined her natural hair colour was similar to the rust colour of Alva's hair. Her voice was softer than Alva's, and her mannerisms were much more feminine. Alva reminded him of Stella physically, but Pete bore herself much more like his fiancée had.

Of course, had Stella had some of the opportunities offered to

Alva, she might have been a very different person.

"It depends on if we're talking about here, or about there?" Pete offered when he didn't pursue it. He smiled. She knew her lore well.

"Yes, basically." He gazed at the mists. How much thicker they had been when he had crossed them, and how warm and welcoming they had felt…

"How long?" Pete pressed.

He sighed. Her stubbornness was definitely akin to his Stella.

"I knew your great-grandmother," he offered. "And I was only gone a week."

He felt old, and too young, and broken again. He'd refused to give his mind the chance to wrap around the meaning of lost time since he'd returned.

To stop now, to focus on what could have been, would surely undo him. He could not afford that.

He glanced back at Alva, who was now only boots peeking out from under her car as she swore heavily. She would have fit in well in the trenches despite her gender, he thought.

"I'm sorry," Pete said.

He turned back to her, surprised again. Her appearance was so distracting that he hadn't expected such kindness from her. He realized how unfair he had been to her, and probably to Alva, and he softened his smile. He was the one out of place here, not them.

"Pete? What does that stand for, anyway?"

She gave him a slight smile in return. “It’s stupid. My real name is Helen, but I liked wearing my hair in pigtails when I was a kid, so my dad called me Pigtail Pete. I never did like the name Helen, anyway. Pete just kinda stuck, I guess, and with dad gone…” She stopped, shifted her stance a bit, re-erected some of her walls.

“So, we’ll be gone from here for how long?” She redirected the conversation.

She was perceptive. And relentless. Hector didn’t see any point in lying to her.

“Probably another hundred years,” he said. “Long enough for the faeries to die out.”

Pete nodded. “And they won’t go back and trap us there.”

“They won’t.” When she gazed at him with that weighing look, he added, “There’s nothing left for them there, anymore.”

He could see a thousand questions light up her eyes, but a flash in the field drew her attention away.

Hector’s blood ran cold as he looked up to see the moon rising too quickly in the day sky, a thin silver sickle. The wind sighed a shimmer of notes - the music of harp strings, flutes tumbling like liquid, the ringing of golden bells.

The sky turned to darkness. The mists sparkled with light from the silver moon.

The land heralded the arrival of royalty.

Chapter 4

AL FELT the shift in the air around her before the darkness and music descended. Her oil pan was almost filled with blood, the scent of iron tangy under the car. Too bad the iron in human blood didn't seem to dissuade the faeries.

Waiting on the last few drops felt like an eternity. Still, she forced herself to wait until the blood was completely drained. Half-assing this job could mean getting stalled again. No more drops fell, so she closed the oil tank and slid out.

A sliver of a moon shone down on her. The fields were dark except for those shimmering mists, which looked like ethereal dancers now, waltzing slowly around them.

She focused on Gruff. "I'm going to bring Percival back down," she said. She clenched the old man's good arm, snapping him to attention. "You start filling up the oil, okay?" Gruff nodded, resolution tightening his features.

He grabbed the oil and headed to front, waiting for her to lower

Percival enough for him to safely prop up the hood. She worked quickly on the jack.

She heard the soft sniffle of her sister's tears over the harps and bells, and she stopped pumping. She would recognize that sound anywhere, having comforted her sister over the loss of their mother, and the death of their father. She went to Pete without thinking about it. She felt as though an invisible hand squeezed her heart, like a faerie wing now lived there and fluttered against every blood vessel.

Pete stood by Hector, the two silhouetted against the light of the moon and the mists, Hector's trench coat and Pete's long hair both motionless. Like a terrible portrait.

She followed her sister's gaze, to where gold-clad knights appeared. Their horses' massive hooves shook the ground, their vibration ringing the bells hanging from their golden bridles.

They moved in a cloud of brightness, as though the world had grown dark just to highlight their magnificence. Behind them, hanging against the sky for a moment, a castle bathed in soft blue light.

Al put her arm around Pete, who cried tears that Al thought she understood. It was beautiful. It was also terrifying.

"We have to go," Hector whispered. Gone was the easy smile that had started to brighten his face.

"Al, I want to go to them," Pete's voice trembled with the exhaustion of staying still. Her voice was just a whisper, but it seemed to travel across the empty fields and reached the knights, who turned toward them.

"I want to go to them," Pete repeated more loudly and took a step forward. Al stepped in front of her, grabbed both of her shoulders hard.

"You stay with me," Al said, and dragged her toward Percival. She swore. The car was still partly jacked up. Gruff had managed to reach into the motor to fill the oil. His height was a hell of an advantage now.

"Get in," Al told Hector. Pete headed for the car, her head lowered.

The sound of harp mixed with a voice, speaking so low that Al couldn't make out the words. But Pete apparently could, and before Al could stop her, she broke at a dead run toward the procession.

Al screamed and ran after her.

The earth churned under her feet, yet Pete felt as though she was flying. Floating above it all, a leaf caught in a summer gale, a seed freed from its flower, a feather somersaulting from a bird in flight. She was floating, she was free, and she just wanted to go faster, faster toward the awaiting knights.

They did not all call to her. Only one spoke to her. Only one knew her heart.

At first, when she'd spotted them, they'd all looked the same. But now she knew better. Their differences were as evident to her as the difference between the sun and the moon. And the second one, with his deep-set eyes, his dark hair, his strong shoulders and jawline, as though ready to take in and fix the world's sorrows… he called to her, above all else.

She had cried, when she'd seen him. Her sister had come, as she always had. But even her warmth wasn't enough. She loved Alva, but Alva meant remembering mom, and dad, and grandma, and everyone who'd left them, one by one. Alva meant feeling the guilt of being useless, of seeing her give up her dreams in favour of

Pete's, as though Pete's were better. More important. Alva ignoring the burns and cuts as she'd laughed off having to learn a trade she hadn't loved at first. Worried about paying rent and putting food on the table.

Alva meant remembering everything Pete had lost, and everything that had been sacrificed for her.

Alva was the past.

But the second knight, whose name tugged silently at her heart, he was the future. He could erase her sorrow and feed her joy instead. She knew it, and she ran faster, his voice so strong on the winds, calling to her very soul, that it almost blocked out Alva's screams for her.

Pete ran faster. Her feet pounded the ground. She could see his eyes now, and his gaze held hers. He waited for her. He knew she would reach him.

Stop following me, she wanted to scream to Alva. *This is my story.* This was hers, and hers alone. This wasn't about her dead parents or her stoic sister. This wasn't about death or sacrifice.

This was the new beginning she knew she wouldn't find at university. Because her past would be there. Her past would always be there.

She wasn't ready to leave for a week and come back a hundred years later to a different landscape. It would still be the same, for her. Her sister would still be stoic. Her parents would still be dead.

And so would the entire world.

She wasn't ready to give up on this world, just yet. But she was willing to give up on herself, if only for a little while.

She reached up and took the extended hand of the knight, and her world became light.

Alva ran so fast that her breath burned in her lungs and her feet kept slipping on the field. She stumbled and fell, pulling herself back up before she'd fully connected with the ground. Roots immediately reached up to trip her.

The closer she'd get to Pete, the more roots pulled free from the ground and snagged her feet. She'd fall, kick, free her feet and get back up, only to fall again.

Rocks caught her, burrowing out from the freshly cultivated ground to cut her. She bled and she stood back up.

She kept running.

She pulled up her feet to avoid tripping, and managed to get close to Pete again before landing on her hand, hard. A rock jabbed her palm and blood gushed out. She pulled the rock out, screamed in frustration and hurled it toward her sister. Maybe she could knock some sense into her.

But the rock just fell daintily to the ground, as though it couldn't bear to hit Pete. As though Pete already belonged to them.

"Pete! Please!" She screamed, her body aching. She did her

best to ignore the pain as she ran. Pete wasn't running so much as floating. For every step she took, she covered the distance of three.

The knights were so close to Pete.

She needed the sand. Hector's sand, which had freed her mind from the faerie.

"Hector!" she cried, her voice hoarse, imagining he was right behind her. She needed him to be right behind her. She didn't dare look, knowing it wouldn't matter unless she first reached Pete.

Al pushed harder, ripping out a root before a thicker root snatched her foot and branches shot out around her. She jumped to the left to avoid the tree erupting out of the ground. Its branches reached for her with crackling fingers, and she barely dodged them.

Another tree burst from the ground beneath her, its thick

branches, dark in the dark day, throwing her several metres away. She landed hard on her side, a rock knocking against her skull.

Blood oozed from her head and she couldn't lift it, seeing her own arms outstretched before her like useless rags.

Pete held out her hand and the knight took it, turning her sister to the purest golden light. Al forced herself to keep looking, to memorize the curve of Pete's outstretched hand, the way her hair shifted to light, the soles of her boots as her legs left the earth. She kept looking despite the blinding light, not bothering to blink away the tears.

If the light scarred her eyes, then she would make sure her sister was the last thing she would see.

"Pete," she whispered, before the light and the pain became unbearable and she heard a sob, not certain if it was hers or Pete's.

Above her, the great tree bloomed pure silver-white.

and over again, like a personal prayer.

"I'm not sure where they are anymore," Hector said, his tense grip hurting his palms.

"Just keep going," Gruff said, still clinging to the dashboard as he scanned the dark horizon. Percival's wheels slid in the mud and bounced up and down over roots writhing out of the ground.

"There!" Gruff shouted, pointing to the left. Hector swung Percival around, screaming as the car slid and the passenger side struck a tree. The watchmaker kept pressing on the gas, the bark scraping Percival's side.

"Go!" Gruff screamed, and Hector joined him in shouting. Percival had certainly earned its name. Hector felt like he was riding a steed of olden times, straight into battle.

Light exploded before them, and Hector lowered his gaze to maintain some of his night vision. Percival's back wheels jerked up, and Hector nearly bit his tongue as they landed hard, narrowly avoiding being tossed up by another sprouting tree.

He headed for the light without hesitation, the engine revving as it engaged a hill.

One of the trees caught Hector's eyes. It had bloomed before any other, its buttery light soothing.

"That's Alva," Gruff said softly, putting his large hand on Hector's arm. Alva was propped against the trunk, silver petals falling on her like a blanket, her rust-coloured hair almost fully out of its braid. Blood dripped from several wounds on her face and arms, and her eyes were closed as though she slept peacefully.

Percival had barely stopped before Hector and Gruff jumped out.

The watchmaker knelt by Alva and put the back of his hand on her cheek. She was still warm to the touch. And she was still breathing.

He began to feel dizzy, the sweet scent of the petals so strong that it crowded out the oxygen.

"Sleeping potion," he managed to say to Gruff. The old man didn't need any further explanation. He leaned down and picked up Alva easily with his good arm, throwing her over his shoulder. Stumbling, Hector followed. Gruff gently placed Alva in the passenger seat. Hector took in deep gulps of fresh air, looking toward the bright light.

Seven knights rode on the golden horses. Seven knights of Faerie who used to protect the queen. Seven knights, who had dedicated their lives to a cause that no longer existed.

And on the second horse, leaning into the golden knight, sat Pete.

"We have to get her," Gruff said, struggling to get in the back seat.

The horses turned away, the orchard continuing to bloom in their path. Flowers erupted on all the trees, their white capturing the silver light of the moon. Petals began to rain down around them, the pollen shimmering in the darkness.

Hector jumped into Percival, fighting the drowsiness.

He glanced at Alva. Gruff looked out the window in awe at the petals, his eyes red from either the potion or tears. They knew that to follow Pete would mean to be caught in the sleeping potion, possibly to never awaken again.

Hector turned Percival and they headed out of the orchard, the petals laying a carpet for their exit.

Chapter 6

THE ROAR of Percival's engine roused Al back to consciousness. She frowned. The car wasn't in the right gear. *Was she driving it?*

The threads of sleep slipped from her mind. She was crumpled in Percival's seat, her back against the door. She wasn't driving. Definitely.

She opened her eyes. Hector gripped the steering wheel tightly, his features equally tight and set.

As though sensing her, he turned to her and gave her a slight smile. "Welcome back," he whispered.

She furrowed her brow. *Welcome back?* Where had she gone? Her head was a cotton factory. She pushed herself up and tried to remember. Outside, the land glowed under a silver moon. To their left, in the distance, danced an orchard of pure petals. She touched her hair, the braid all messy. Petals were still trapped in the tangles. She pulled them out and they evaporated to shining dust.

She'd been under one of those trees.

"Pete!" she cried out, her voice dry and strained. "Where's Pete?" She turned around. Gruff reached up from the back seat to hold her shoulders and calm her down.

Except Al didn't want to be calm.

"Where the hell is she?" she demanded, focusing on Hector. The watchmaker slowed down and stopped the car before turning to face her. His movements were deliberate, weighed down by the knowledge he had to impart.

Al closed her eyes, images pouncing on her awakening mind. Pete, running away, outlined by the silver of the moon. The knight's hand, extending. Her sister's slender hand reaching up, reaching for him… She opened her eyes, wishing it had all been a dream.

"He has her," she said, more to herself than Hector, who nodded anyway.

"Well, how the hell do we get her back?" Her tone clearly implied that she expected an answer. That she expected him to know how to save her sister. And not to consider arguing that she couldn't be saved.

Gruff's hand was still on her shoulder, and it grounded her. But it also reminded her of Gretchen, vanishing into the air, becoming mist… Grief worked its way up her throat, but she pushed it back down.

"We're getting her back," she stated, welcoming no argument.

Hector nodded and looked sideways, as though working out the problem.

"We can go to the faerie world still," he offered, hesitantly.

"And leave Pete behind?" Al snapped.

"No." Hector held up both hands defensively, as though fearful Al might slug him. Which she was considering. He continued, "I mean, she's probably there already."

"Why the hell would the knights go there? I thought you said the faeries had deserted their land for ours."

"Well, yes, but those aren't faeries per say," he grimaced, either trying to simplify what he was trying to say, or working on a lie. He sighed and lowered his hands. "Look, it's not as simple as any of us would like. But those were the faerie queen's own guards, her own knights. They're powerful enough to travel to and from the world. If Pete was taken by one, they would go back there."

"What do you mean, *if*?" Al practically jumped on him.

"I mean, if they - dear Lord help me - if they keep her." His features seemed to drain of all colour in the silver light, but still he met Alva's eyes. He reached out and took her hands in his. She almost ripped them away, but his gaze held her steady.

"Did she run into them, or was she beckoned?" His voice was as steady as his eyes.

"She was beckoned," she said, remembering Pete's unwavering run toward them, the hand reaching down…

"Then she's safe. The knight…" He paused, held her hand more tightly as though bracing her or stopping her from hitting him.

He was stronger than he looked, but she knew that if she got mad enough, she could beat him to a bloody pulp. Especially with Big Bertha.

Except she wasn't angry. She felt drained, and crushed. She'd had one job, to keep her sister safe.

And she'd failed.

"Is it like the old stories? Tam-Lin and that bunch?" Al whispered. She'd read Pete the stories after their dad had passed. Al had read until Pete would drift off to sleep, sealing Pete's love of them so firmly that she had slept surrounded by the books and had wanted to study them for the rest of her life.

"I'm afraid so," Hector answered. "But we can still get to her."

Al nodded and pulled her hands free, suddenly wanting to be very much alone.

"Let's go, then. To the faerie world." Gruff squeezed her shoulder and let her go. Hector focused back on driving the car. Alva was so trapped in her own thoughts that she didn't wince when he ground Percival's gears.

The knight had taken Pete to become his wife.

And to bear a child.

Unless she could get to her in time, Pete would never be the same again. She might already be too late.

Al leaned her forehead against the window and watched her breath fog the glass, fracturing the silver moonlight.

Chapter 7

IT TOOK all of five jerky minutes of driving before Al ordered Hector to pull over and let her drive. She looked out her cracked windshield, the steering wheel warm and familiar in her hands. He hadn't argued and, in fact, had looked quite relieved. Gruff snored softly in the back.

Fenelon Falls lay less than an hour away. Alva passed the time by trying to calculate the speed of the horses. They had vanished after the orchard had erupted into blooms. But they were faeries, or at least faerie-touched. Who knew how fast they could travel?

But, say they were still there but only invisible, then a horse could travel, what… five kilometers an hour? Was that too much? She had no clue. She dealt in cars, not in every available mode of transportation.

"Do horses travel five kilometres per hour?" Alva asked Hector. The watchmaker looked at her, bleary-eyed. He'd been on the verge of sleep.

"What?" He asked, yawning.

"Horses. How fast do they travel?"

"Real horses, or magical ones?"

"Fine, I'm an easy read. I was just wondering. Think we'll beat them to the faerie world?"

He readjusted himself in his seat, staring straight ahead.

"Maybe," he offered simply. She sighed.

"Fine. We'll find her, though." She paused. "I don't think I've thanked you, yet. So, you know, thank you."

He turned to look at her, eyebrows lifted in surprise.

"Why would you thank me?"

She shrugged. "Well, you saved me back at the shop. And you came for Pete and me, and you're sticking it out with us, trying to keep us safe." She managed to give him a small smile. "So, thanks for that. I'm sorry I hit you with Big Bertha."

"That did rather smart," he said, gently touching the back of his head and wincing. "But you're most welcome."

Al was quiet for a few more moments, but the silence, now that it had been broken, proved too stifling.

"You loved her," she said, not certain how to word the question.

But he understood her. "I did. Very much." He pulled out her great-grandmother's watch and touched the front of the cover. He saw her looking at him and gave her an apologetic smile. "I meant to give this back to you before now…" He handed her the watch.

She shook her head. "You can keep it. For now."

He looked grateful and curled his fingers around the watch, as though it were his most prized possession. And she supposed it was.

"How long were you trapped there? About a century, I guess?"

He nodded, looking down at the watch. She didn't think he'd say anything else, but then he did, opening up the watch and staring at its still hands.

"It's strange, coming back to a world that kept moving along without you. You think your life made an impact, and then you vanish and you're not even a memory. A hundred years just… lost." He stopped, his head lowered, his brown hair not hiding his despair.

"You weren't forgotten," Al said, reaching over and squeezing his hand. He looked up. "The watch was passed down for three generations, and it's the greatest family treasure we own. If my great-grandmother had forgotten you, wouldn't she have lost this watch? Along with all of its promises and hopes?"

He weighed her words for a few moments and then nodded. She let go of his hand, feeling awkward again. Gruff wasn't snoring anymore, but he certainly wasn't saying anything.

"Thank you," Hector said, and after that, the silence lay a bit more comfortably on the car.

The road split in two up ahead, and Alva slowed down to turn right. A sign caught her attention. It was green, like most road signs in this area.

"That's not right," she said as she approached. The arrows for Fenelon Falls were pointing east, and not north, which is where they needed to go. She knew this area like the back of her hand.

"What's not right?" Hector said, sitting up and alert.

"The sign," just as she said it, the car spun around. The steering wheel was steady in her hand, the motor revving as the wheels hovered over the ground. They all screamed as they were thrown around like a carnival ride from hell, the world blurring around them. Then Percival connected with the ground with a jerk. Al pounded on the brakes while she regained her bearings. She was dizzy and slightly nauseated.

"Al..." Gruff warned from the back. She opened her eyes again

and pushed past the dizziness. She gasped. The landscape had changed. The moon shone perfectly above them, surrounded by darkness, the sky below it exploding into electric colours where sat four suns, each low on opposing horizons.

The road had split into ten, and Percival was in the perfect centre. Each road drew a perfect line away from them and were spaced evenly – a perfect geometric pattern.

She looked at her compass on the dashboard. The arrow was spinning itself silly.

"Some faeries have a nasty sense of humour," Hector offered as an explanation.

"Well, I'm running out of mine. Which way do we go?"

Hector looked at the roads, examining each carefully.

"Hector," Alva said after a few moments, "we need to get Pete. Now." Hector nodded and exited the car. Al looked back at Gruff, whose eyes were tightly shut. He must have hit his arm while spinning.

"Gruff?" She asked.

"I'm okay." The pain in his voice was evident. She wished she could do more to help then giving him more pain killers and water.

She stepped outside to follow Hector. A whole new world greeted her. The air was thick with perfume and rich with the sounds of harp. Near and far, the music seemed to come from every pore of the earth.

"Bloody faeries and their soundtracks," she muttered.

Between each road lay a patch of grass, adorned with uniquely coloured flowers. Pink, lavender, blue, yellow, orange, black.

Alva stood stiffly, blood pumping, wishing she could direct her fears toward an answer. Hector crouched near a road, then another. He seemed as lost as she was.

Her heart bumped in her throat, then in her head, blood slamming against the back of her eyes. Shimmering petals rode the breeze around her. Alva held her breath until they'd passed, gliding toward one of the sunsets.

"Hector," Al prodded.

He stood up, running his hand through his hair in frustration.

"I don't know, Alva." He flushed, as though surprised by his own lack of patience, then cleared his throat. "I'm not sure. Obviously the flowers are a clue, but I don't know which way leads where. I'm not even certain that the clue is for us."

"Hector, you got us off the bridge with that sand. Would it help now?"

He hesitated, then spoke apologetically. "I barely have any left."

Al placed herself right in front of him. He was just a bit taller than her, so she could look him in the eye.

"We need to get Pete, Hector." She softened her voice, her heart thumping less wildly now. Still, she fought against the encroaching grief.

"Please."

He looked dejected, as though he'd failed in his greatest mission yet. "I only have enough to test one road. If we put it on and it stays, it's the right road. If not… we've wasted the sand."

"Can't we just reuse it?" Al wished the world made sense again. Of course, if it did, she'd be at work right now, probably fixing a faulty carburetor. Which would be just fine with her.

Hector shook his head. "Not once it touches human soil. Then it loses its magical properties." He glanced toward one of the sunset, the light reflected in his brown eyes. "Things can't necessarily easily travel from one world to the next."

"All right then. We pick our road." She looked around carefully to each road. Every single one was flanked by two lengths of grass and flowers. So every road represented two colours. She frowned.

"Okay, how the hell do we pick a road?"

"I depends how they were formed. That's the trickster's game."

"So they were formed based on us? Is that it?"

Hector looked around. "I guess so. No one else is trapped here. So, they're taking our utmost desires and transplanting them here."

"Great," Alva mumbled. "Well, that would be Pete, right?"

"It should be. But, remember, It could reflect any or all of us. We have no way of knowing."

"That lack of specificity is really useful, thanks," Al mumbled.

She turned around slowly again. The white could be Gretchen. The green flowers could be Gruff's son, an army man. Gruff hadn't talked about his desires, but she guessed the road flanked between both those colours was for him. She glanced back at the car. Her friend and mentor still stared at a ray of sunset, his features even paler.

She focused back on the roads. Hector was a mystery to her. He was out of his time and seemed out of his world. He'd loved her great-grandmother, but Alva couldn't begin to guess the colours that spurred him on. As though reading her mind, Hector spoke.

"I want Pete back too, Alva. I promised your great-grandmother that I'd always look after our children, once we were married." He held her gaze as he spoke. "And, even though I never got to marry her—" He swallowed hard and lowered his voice until it was almost lost in the gentle strumming of the harp. "I still intend to keep that promise. To save you, and Pete. It's why I came back, and I don't intent to fail."

Al nodded slowly. His unspoken words smothered every other

sound, and she had to break eye contact, unable to consolidate his grief with her own. She turned to the black flowers. Black, like her sister's hair and clothing. Red flowers on the other side. Red, like love. Probably like the flowers Hector had given Stella Alwilda at one point, a long time ago.

One the other side of the black patch were yellow flowers. A yellow she'd only seen bloom one other place - on a rosebush by the side of road near a lake and an abandoned school bus.

Molly.

Al didn't know if it was because Molly was the unofficial third sister, or if it was because Molly had somehow found a way to bring Al and Pete back together again. Because that's what she always did. On Molly's other side were rust flowers, like Al's hair. There was a road just for her, too. But none for Molly.

She couldn't speak, just then, the lump in her throat too thick for sound to form around it. But she could point, and she did. Hector saw the black and the yellow, the painfully distinct hair colours. He glanced at the road that could be Al's and looked at her questioningly.

"Pete's road," Al said, her voice cracking. "I'll always choose Pete's road."

Hector nodded and shoved his hand in his coat pocket. He had so little sand left that he had to turn his pocket inside out and shake it onto the road.

The sky flickered to darkness, then back to light, and then turned

off completely. The harp ended, the air smothering and thick. Alva couldn't see the tip of her nose.

She reached out and found Hector's hand. She held it and waited, her wide-open eyes unable to break any of the inky blackness.

A heartbeat passed. And another.

She inhaled and exhaled slowly.

She held Hector's hand but didn't move closer to him, and neither did he come closer to her. They were rooted in place either by fear or by anticipation. Maybe both.

A heartbeat.

A breath.

She imagined the sands of time slip through her fingers and into the watchmaker's hand.

Chapter 8

GRUFF WAITED in the back seat. He didn't move, barely breathed. His sixty-six years of age had taught him not to blink, and he certainly didn't fear death. No, what he feared was leaving Al alone. His own children hadn't needed him for a long time, but Al and Pete still needed someone.

The darkness encroached on everything, even his thoughts. He could still feel Percival's seat under him, but couldn't see it. His arm throbbed and a pain had been growing in his chest, a tightness he feared but didn't fight against. What could he do? Make Al forget her sister in a quest to save him? How could she?

The world was ending, and he was okay with not being along for the ride.

"You could have vanished with your wife," a voice said. It barely carried in a darkness so thick that it smothered sound.

Gruff didn't answer. He wasn't sure what to say, and he'd long ago decided that speaking just for the sake of it was a waste of energy. Addressing disembodied voices in the dark seemed like a horrible idea, anyhow.

So he waited.

The voice grew impatient. Gruff couldn't tell if it was a man or a woman who spoke, the voice both sharp toned and deep. "Why didn't you leave with your wife? Did you not love her enough?"

Gruff took a deep breath and closed his eyes despite the darkness. Had he loved her enough? He wasn't sure. He had, once. He still loved her presence, maybe more than her being. He hated being alone.

He still didn't answer. Seconds passed by, accompanied by his irregular heartbeats.

"I could bring you to her."

Gruff knew in that moment that he had loved his wife. And that he needed to let Al be free and stop worrying about an old injured man.

Still, he didn't answer.

His heart beat his decision with a now regular rhythm. Except Gruff feared, deep in the panicked trenches of his feverish mind, that it was no longer his own heart beating in his chest.

After her mother's departure, Al's father had given her a nightlight to ward off the darkness. In that darkness, Al always imagined she could see the outline of her mother, coming to soothe her, to comfort her, to hold her and take the nightmares away. Pete was too little to remember their mother, but Al remembered. Sort of. She mostly just remembered her outline. The promise of hope.

In the darkness, her mother had been like a saviour. In the light, the sadness she carried with her like a blanket stole the colour from her surroundings. So her dad had tried to make everything brighter by being funnier, more engaged, more loving… but in the darkness, it was her mother that Al called for.

Al bit her lip, the old instincts crowding her mind with fear.

The darkness around her began to lift just a tiny bit, enough to show her an outline. Such a familiar outline, of someone she knew.

Someone she loved.

Someone she hadn't seen for a long time.

The outline of her mother turned some of the darkness to gray, easing Al's fears. She held her arms out to Al, as though she would hold her and steal away the nightmares. Hector squeezed her hand so hard that it hurt, and she looked away from her mother to him. He wasn't looking at her, though. He was looking at another woman, wearing a long dress, her hair properly pinned up under a hat.

Alva knew she stared at her great-grandmother, Stella Alwilda Taverner. She felt the pang of regret flow from Hector through her like electricity, and she held his hand tightly, to keep him from going after her.

She looked around, hearing only her own breath in the lifting darkness. No, the darkness wasn't lifting. The figures were simply slightly lighter in their various shades of gray, tones splattered like a burst of colour in their monochrome world.

She saw people she didn't know surrounding her, probably hopes from Gruff or Hector. She didn't see her father anywhere, and felt she'd betrayed him for wanting her mother to remove the darkness, even though mom had left them all so long ago.

She saw Gretchen in a long flowing robe, the same one she had vanished in. She hoped Gruff was still in the car, that he was sleeping. Dreaming. That he'd be spared the sight.

Then she glanced at her mother again. She forced her eyes to keep moving and then, between mom and Stella, she spotted Pete.

Shorter than Al, her dark hair blending almost perfectly into the night. Pete stood quietly, as unmoving and expressionless as the rest of them. Faceless, really. Only an outline, or a shadow.

A hope. Or an illusion.

"Pete," Alva said. The word slammed into the empty sky like a hammer, and the darkness shattered and crumbled around them. The sun broke through and Alva's eyes watered, but she refused to take her eyes off Pete.

The figures turned to black mist and evaporated. Behind where Pete had been standing lay the road to Fenelon Falls, revealed again in the sunlight, the illusion vanquished.

Al looked at Percival. The orange muscle car was aimed at a tree. If she'd so much as nudged forward, she would have hit it. She spotted Gruff. His features were pale and tight.

"We should go," Al said, tugging gently on Hector's arm.

His body turned toward her, but he kept his gaze on where Stella had been just moments before.

"Hector, we have to find Pete," she said. That seemed to snap him out of it and he slowly turned to her.

"The worse part of faeries," he whispered, not letting go of her hand just yet, "is that they see desires in us that we ourselves don't even understand. It gives them power unlike any other."

Al squeezed his hand. "It's sunny now," she said and cocked her head toward Percival.

He smiled a bit more brightly. "It is. Let's go."

Chapter 9

THE ROAD stretched before Alva. She sun warmed her gently, and she began to feel a bit normal again. Like this would be over, soon. They would reach the faerie world and then they could rest. And Pete would be there. And they'd laugh away a hundred years.

She was growing impatient, but calmed at the sight of the shimmering water to her left. She began to smile, then cold dread washed over her.

"Hector?" Alva whispered urgently.

His head snapped up. "What is it?"

She pointed to the left. "There's not supposed to be water here."

"Go faster,!" he ordered, peering at the encroaching water. It neared the road up ahead. Al pressed on the gas, the speedometer's needle moving up in a steady motion as she went well above the posted speed limit.

120 km/hour...

130…

140…

"Faster, Alva!" Hector screamed. "If we're caught in that, we don't stand a chance!"

She didn't bother telling him she couldn't accelerate any faster, the gas pedal all the way to the floor, the car already in fifth gear. She just concentrated on driving, willing Percival to somehow go faster.

Fenelon Falls was just ahead, the turn to enter the town barely a kilometre away. The water drew ever nearer on the left-hand side of the car. There were other vehicles on the road, some abandoned, others with occupants in them. Some people were just standing by their cars, taking pictures of the growing pool of water. Alva honked as Percival roared past them. She wanted to scream at them to move, but she didn't dare lower her window. The last time she was near water, it hadn't turned out so great.

The sky grew dark and cloudy. A song played on the winds, and Hector sat straight in his seat, peering around for the next attack. Alva focused on the road, on going straight, on not hitting any gawkers or abandoned cars, on just… getting to the falls.

Getting to Pete.

She could hear the song now, a low voice in a language she didn't understand. Alva jumped as sheets of rain suddenly pummeled Percival's hood. Rain accumulated quickly, swelling the lake, giving Alva no time to compensate her driving or slow down.

Water slammed into their side and the wheels lifted from the road.

Alva tried to turn, to maintain control, but the car jerked forward into the rising current, water gushing through the bottoms of the door.

Lightning split the sky and Al saw creatures swimming around Percival. They had wild hair of algae, sharp teeth, and glowing slit-eyes. Al swore and Hector grabbed her arm to calm her down.

"It's okay. This isn't too bad," he said, giving her a tight smile.

"Are you insane?" Al screamed at him, but the winds died down and the waters retreated. Percival made contact with the road again. The motor was still running, but Al wasn't pressing on the gas. The car idled forward and would have stalled, but she regained her senses and popped the gearshift back into first. The water retreated from everywhere, including inside the car and the engine.

She didn't speed up. The ground was covered in gold and jewels, shining even under the cloud cover. Percival's wheels crunched as they went over more riches than Al had ever seen.

"What the heck are they doing?" She asked, still creeping forward, too terrified or mesmerized to go any faster.

"A trap. They're laying a trap. Once enough people are gathering the jewels, they'll spring it."

"And?" Al asked, not sure she really wanted to know.

"They'll eat them."

"Oh." She pressed harder on the gas and shifted up, careful not to go too fast for fear of swerving on a pile of gold. A laugh bubbled in her chest and she wanted to make a joke to Gruff about the towing calls they could get about "gold-induced crashes." But the laughter died just as quickly as it had come. Gruff was still passed out on the back seat.

Some cars were stopping on the road as she neared the entrance to town. Behind her, she could see people nabbing jewels and gold.

"How stupid are these people?" She asked, disgusted. With herself, for not warning them, and with them, for falling for such an obvious trap.

"They think this is still temporary, Alva. They think maybe that this is a payoff for whatever they've lost. We're taught that we're to be given tests in life, and if we pass them, we receive a reward. They just think this is their reward."

"Well, I still think they're stupid," Al mumbled, wishing her feet were dry. Lightning crashed and she heard screams behind her. She saw a whole family swooped up by a long arm.

"Just keep driving," Hector said, before Alva could ask what was happening.

She didn't argue.

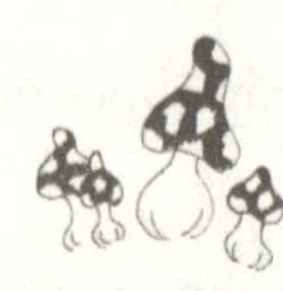

The sign for Fenelon Fall was askew and blood-covered. Before having passed the first house, Al saw two bodies decapitated by the side of the road. Hector stared around the car, eagle-eyed.

"How bad is this going to be?" Al asked. The falls weren't far, but neither had the town been before a river had tried to sweep them away.

"I'm hoping most of the creatures will have moved on, chasing the escaping villagers," he said. "This is close to a major entry point to the faerie world. The faeries here might be more dangerous."

"More dangerous? That's hard to believe."

Hector stared at the outline of a burnt man on the side of a house.

"Believe it."

Al nodded and focused on not hitting any debris. Percival rolled over what looked like an arm, and she winced. At least there hadn't been a body attached to it.

"We'll find Pete through the falls," she said as a mantra, keeping her goal in mind. She ran over another arm. This one still had most of a person attached.

"Yes, we will," Hector said.

A scream bounced off the nearby houses before someone landed right in front of Percival, with a sickening thud. Another scream,

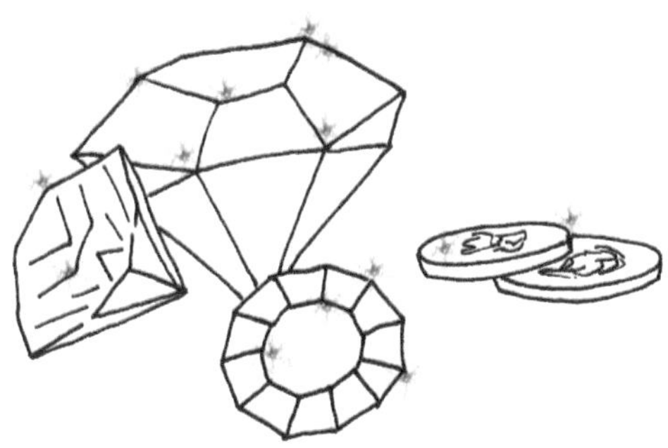

and someone else fell on their left.

"Hector," Al said. It wasn't supposed to rain people.

"Just keep going," he whispered, glancing up. "Faster. Faster."

Al closed her eyes as she went over the person who had landed right in front of them. Another person landed on a nearby roof, and shingles flew onto the road. The sudden end to the screams made Al's stomach kick.

She kept going, no more bodies falling. For now. Hector stopped staring up and leaned back in his seat

"They're gone," he said.

Al was about to ask what "they" had been when she stopped. A wave of screaming people were running and toward them in a mad dash for safety. Some were barefoot, others partly nude. Their faces were wrapped in terror. Al stared as one woman clung to a child, lost her footing, and went down.

On some faces she could now see blood. And she could feel their terror. They were coming up on them fast.

"Quick, get down," Hector instructed, pulling on her. She undid her seatbelt and slid down just under the dash, as much as she could. Hector did the same on his side. Gruff was already so low that no one should spot him.

The panicked throng reached the car, some slamming into it. Others banged right on top of Percival.

Then the screams began. And the laughter, the horrible laughter...

Al heard a shriek right beside Percival and then something

thudded against her car. She closed her eyes and tried not to imagine what was happening a thin car door away. Another scream, and then the entire crowd erupted in wails, like a cap exploding off a shaken bottle. And through it all she could sense their fear, like an electric current.

She tried to push herself further under the steering wheel, the pedals against her legs.

Pete. She was safe away from here. She was already in the faerie world, and she'd used all that great folklore knowledge to negotiate some sort of safety. To ensure she wouldn't be hurt before Alva found her. She knew Al would come for her. Al always came.

The screams blanketed the world and then, in an instant, were gone. Everything grew quiet again, muffled into complete silence. Al opened her eyes and looked at Hector. He was pale, and his hand shook slightly as he pushed himself back up. She did the same, fearing she was going to puke. The car stank of iron, and the windows were layered with blood.

Fog enveloped her mind. She needed to turn the car on and clean the windshield. She needed to see to reach the falls. She thought these things, but her hand didn't move toward the ignition.

Something landed on Percival's hood. She looked to Hector, his wide eyes filled with the same terror she felt.

Before either could move, someone began wiping the windshield. Al watched the slow, deliberate movement of a piece of a fabric, turning from white to red as it absorbed the blood.

A gaunt arm held the fabric—a hat, she could see now. An old man stood on her hood, his body more skin and bone than muscle. He put the bloodied hat on his head and smiled, showing pointed teeth. Then he looked down and saw Alva.

He threw himself at her, jerking her out of her fog. She spun the tires, trying to start too quickly, and the old man slid off the blood-slickened hood and fell in front of the car. Alva ran him over and kept going, smashing into the side of a car before backing up, running over the old man again.

Hector was holding the dashboard for safety, struggling to get his seatbelt on.

"Are you all right?" he asked. She nodded quickly and focused on the road.

Three blocks later, they could see the falls.

The water glistened, unheeding of the gray day. The dry lightning reflected off it, giving it blue tints. The falls followed a bed of concrete, but they still came from a natural source. Hector had told her it would work fine. That water was water.

She stopped the car as near as she could get, on a bridge just above the rushing waters. They'd have to go down the stairs with Gruff and then hop over the metal guard that stopped people from falling in. But they were near. She could feel the humidity infiltrating the car.

Alva glanced at the bushes lining the path and wanted to throw up.

"I'll go ahead and scout," Hector said. "Get whatever you need ready to go. I'll come back and we can both carry Gruff across."

Alva hesitated and then nodded.

"Watch your back," she whispered.

He looked as though he wanted to say something, but then he just nodded and slipped away.

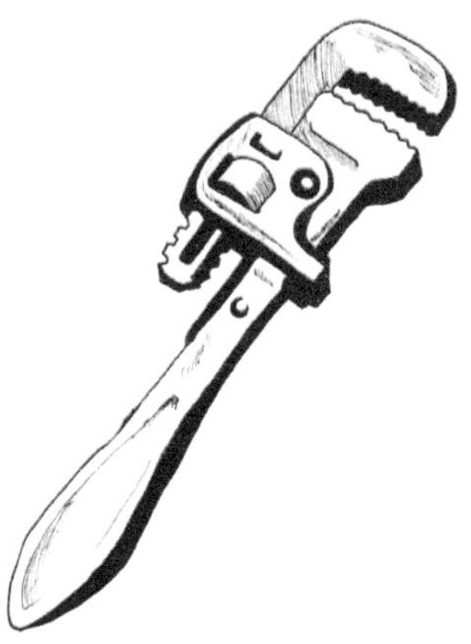

Chapter 10

HECTOR VANISHED around the corner, to the side of the bridge, where two bushes hid him from her view. She imagined the path, lined with bittersweet nightshade bushes, red berries dull in the gray day, the steps turning three ways before he would reach bottom.

Then, a hop over the guardrail and they could go into the water.

The air was fresh here, the falls kicking up the scent of lilies of the valley. As long as she ignored the smell of iron on Percival, anyway. Her beautiful orange car was now brownish red, and there were things stuck in its wheels that she didn't want to think about.

She needed to get ready. She had no idea what to bring, but it wasn't like she had a lot to choose from. The few emergency supplies she kept in Percival would have to do.

But this was hardly a "stuck in the snow overnight" type of emergency, so she felt ridiculously unprepared. She reached the back of Percival, also slick with blood. She didn't want to touch it with her hand, so she kicked it. The trunk popped open.

She grabbed some tools, water and extra blankets, and left the trunk open, afraid of making too much noise. She didn't want to draw any more attention than necessary. Who knew what else lurked here?

She secured Big Bertha to her belt and was ready. She'd wait until Hector was back to move Gruff, who was still feverish and passed out. She wasn't weak by any standard, but Gruff wasn't small by any standard, either.

She glanced around. Nothing moved on the street. To the south, where they'd come from, the dry lightning still danced. She wondered if the trap had been tripped, all those people swept away and consumed.

She looked down, to the shops lining the main street. It was a cute downtown, with multi-coloured buildings and signs. Most of the windows were broken, but she couldn't see any bodies here. Cars had been abandoned. She stared at a high heel shoe tipped over in the middle of the road, guessing the person had gone for an unwanted flight.

The flowerpots hanging off the decorative lampposts shimmered in the gray light. Al took a careful step forward. There were fireflies, or something that looked like them, dancing around the flowers. The pink flowers seemed to be growing under the hospice of the creatures, the vine reaching further down and the flowers swelling with beauty.

Al took a step back. Just because it was beautiful hardly meant it wasn't deadly. They'd all learned that lesson the hard way.

She went back to Percival and waited. Even with the car covered in blood, Al felt a pang of regret at having to leave her old beast behind. It had been her first big repair jobwith her dad. She'd spent hours on it, learning a lifetime of knowledge and refining her skills. Percival had taken hits for her. He'd driven her and Pete home after their dad's funeral. He'd helped them move into their tiny apartment.

He'd been an awesome car. And now she was abandoning him to rust and decay.

A hundred years.

Such a long time. Al wondered what it would all look like by the time she and Pete returned. The shops would be crumbling, grown over with vines. Maybe trees, even. The bodies would be bones, if they hadn't completely vanished. The streets broken by roots and

vegetation, nature reclaiming this part of the world.

And no one would be here to remember what it had looked like. All the hopes and dreams planted in this town, probably this world, would be gone and forgotten. Withered, no matter how much they had once bloomed.

Nothing would be the same.

And it didn't matter. All that mattered was that they were safe.

She looked at the clock. Hector had been gone five minutes.

Five minutes wasn't that long, but the falls were one minute away, and she was certain he was moving fast. She hesitated. Should she go after him and help him if he needed it? Should she just wait with Gruff?

And what would she do without Hector? He'd been her guide, and she was starting to think of him as her friend.

Al snatched up Big Bertha, finding comfort in the cold metal.

Hector crouched by a bush, trapped by the monster now standing on the steps just above him, still mostly hidden by the foliage. He was lucky it hadn't spotted him on his first pass. Covered in fur, the large creature possessed only single body parts. One hand, one leg, one eye. All were placed in a centre line running down the front of its body. It would have been comical had it not proved so terrifying. In its hand, it held a club, blood and bits of flesh trapped between the spikes.

It knew Hector was near. It was aware of his presence on some primordial level, anyway. Hector wished he knew its weakness. He'd only spent a week in the faerie land, and there were too many faeries for him to have met them all. Plus, they didn't all court the faerie queen who had held him prisoner.

He had done what he could, he reminded himself, trying to blend in further with the bush. Sometimes, he found himself missing the trenches. At least then he had known who his enemy was and, for the most part, where they were.

The creature shifted, sniffed the air. Hector couldn't see its nose, lost in the dark matted fur. Its hand twitched, the spiked club moving sideways in anticipation.

Hector held his breath and looked closer, to see what the creature had spotted.

His heart dropped when he saw Alva coming down the steps to look for him.

Alva carefully walked down the steps. The hairs on the back of her neck were electrified. Her boots made no noise on the ground, and she walked in a crouch, Big Bertha held tightly in her hands.

A bush rustled to the right and she turned to look just as Hector exploded from below the steps.

"Alva, down!" he screamed, and she threw herself back, holding on to the wrench as if her life depended on it. A spiked club swung centimetres from her head. She felt the heat of its passing, and some of her hair tangled in it and was ripped from her scalp. She didn't hesitate, scrambling up to get away as the club came down again, barely missing her leg.

She bounded up the stairs, but the creature wasn't far behind. She could hear it jumping after her. She had to get to Percival, but the car seemed so impossibly far… the creature knocked her from behind, and she fell to the ground and rolled into the base of a tree. Her side hurt where she'd been hit, but she forced herself to keep moving as quickly as she could.

Which wasn't quickly enough.

The club came down and caught her left leg. It just grazed it, but her pants were shredded and her skin ripped.

She cried out and grabbed Big Bertha, intent on at least trying to make a final stand.

Alva stood in front of the creature, managing to evade a hit and striking it with her wrench, but she landed hard on her wounded leg.

Hector scrambled after them. He had no weapon, save one.

He ripped off his boot, then looked up to the sky for one brief moment, not afraid of death.

He'd been dead before.

He pulled off his boot, ripped the sole and hurled it at the creature, the sand arching and striking the creature. It shrieked, unable to reconcile the magic from its people in this earthly realm.

Hector tried to remain standing, but the pain was already getting the better of him. He cried and fell to the ground, screaming for Alva to get to the falls, to go beyond them.

To be safe.

The creature stumbled and fell, its round mouth forming a perfect "o" as Hector's boot hit it in the back of its head, the sand sprinkling like sparkles everywhere.

Hector's sand.

She heard him scream, saw him fall. She ignored the fallen monster and ran to his side.

She held him in her arms. His head was turning white, threads of silver conquering his brown hair. His face seemed to be falling into itself as wrinkles pressed against his brow. His hand reached for hers, gaunt and thin, fingers that had so carefully worked on the smallest gears now impossibly bony.

His eyes jutted out of his face, which sagged against his skull.

He was gaining a hundred years before her eyes.

"Go," he whispered.

She didn't hesitate as she threw his withering body over her shoulder. With Big Bertha in her other hand, she ran back up the steps, ignoring the pain in her side and leg.

She wasn't leaving anyone else behind! Molly, Pete… no, this was it. They were making it to the faerie land.

She was winded by the time she reached Percival, but she ignored her burning lungs. She could feel Hector become lighter, as though turning to the dust his body should already be.

She ignored that, too, and dropped him in the trunk, slamming it shut. She wiped the blood on her pants and threw herself into the front seat, turning on the car. There was no more time for ceremony, for gentleness, or for hesitation. The pink flowers practically shone now, and the tiny faeries danced wildly around them, as though excited by Alva's determination.

Al backed up until she was well past the creature. She glanced back. Gruff had one eye open.

"I'm either going to save us or I'm going to kill us, Gruff," Al said, more out of confession than in asking for guidance.

Still, she felt ridiculously relieved when he held up his hand weakly and a crooked right thumb was held up. The ground beneath her shook, and she didn't hesitate.

She slammed into first and drove straight for the stairs. The only way to clear them was to jump them. She headed straight for the monster, popping her gears right before hitting it in an effort to push up her front wheels. Her gamble worked, and the wheels spun over the creature, catapulting Percival over the stairs.

Alva's bum left her seat and she heard a thunk that could only be Hector in the trunk. At least he wasn't dust yet.

Percival tipped down, its nose losing altitude. They were just over the falls. But there was no way she could turn the car, not in mid air, to cross the water. They were going to crash, and a scream burst out of her.

As though answering her call, the small faeries gathered around Percival, turning dark shades of pink as they plastered themselves around the car.

Time turned slowly and seemed to stop. Like Stella Alwilda's watch. Like the world around them.

Al closed her eyes and waited for impact.

Epilogue

EVERY BLADE of grass held a memory.

On every tree, stone and petal was etched the knowledge of origins, of purpose, of hope. Doorways that only a few could travel, before the veils grew too thick to cross and his people were trapped on the other side. So many.

An entire kingdom.

Forged in the first stone of this planet, from the angriest volcanoes that had become the richest continents, the spires of the castle lay crumbling, stones falling away like leaves in the wind. Those that struck the ground did so in silence. Even sound shunned the faded land. The throne room lay empty, save for a whisper, an echo of a final lament.

A plea for time to leave them be. For stones to hold fast. For fear to be re-forged into something that does not burn as quickly: acceptance.

But the watchmaker had refused to assist. He was gone, now,

like so many of them. Gone running off in search of vengeance, or a new land, or again, that elusive quality the faerie queen had despised most of all, even in her final days when she could have benefited most from it.

Hope.

The faerie prince walked across the stone path that crumbled from recent overuse. Bluebells drooped near it, fading, trampled by uncaring feet. He gently scooped up one and tried to prop it, but its petals slipped into his palm.

He looked to the once blue sky speckled with darkness, and grief threatened to overpower him. Then a sound erupted in his silent kingdom. He turned where a colony of dark pink faeries broke away and flew up. He smiled.

"You came back."

But they slid away again, back through the falls, the doors closing behind them. His smile became as faded as his kingdom.

They'd left something behind.

An orange beast had slid through. One of those infernal machines from the human world.

The prince watched and waited. A stone fell near the machine, a great tower teetering over it. No one moved within the beast.

He did not care. He simply waited, as still as the world around him.

The world would crumple into despair, and he only hoped it would sweep him away before its final cry.

- The End of Nigh 2 -

The Tale Continues

Nigh 3

Other books by Marie Bilodeau

Heirs of a Broken Land

Princess of Light

Warrior of Darkness

Sorceress of Shadows

Destiny

Destiny's Blood

Destiny's Fall

Destiny's War

www.mariebilodeau.com

www.ingramcontent.com/pod-product-compliance
Lightning Source LLC
Chambersburg PA
CBHW021623030826
48979CB00036B/1891/J

* 9 7 8 0 9 9 4 0 4 3 9 5 5 *